Peep!

Kevin Luthardt

PEACHTREE
ATLANTA

For Alicia,
my wife and my best friend.

Thank you Jesus, my Lord and Savior.

—K. L.

Published by
PEACHTREE PUBLISHERS, LTD.
1700 Chattahoochee Avenue
Atlanta, Georgia 30318-2112

www.peachtree-online.com

Manufactured in China

Book design by Kevin Luthardt
Composition by Loraine M. Joyner

10 9 8 7 6 5 4 3 2 1
First Edition

Library of Congress Cataloging-in-Publication Data

Luthardt, Kevin.
    Peep! / by Kevin Luthardt.
        p. cm.
    Summary: Although a boy is lonely after the hatchling duckling that followed him home finally joins other ducks, he soon meets another creature.
    ISBN 1-56145-046-4
    [1. Ducks—Fiction. 2. Pets—Fiction. 3. Stories without words—Fiction.] I. Title.
    PZ7.L9793 Pe 2003
    [E]—dc21
                                                    2002035910